SNUGGLEBUG BOOKS ™

Who Is Sleeping?

Written by
Andrew Gutelle

Illustrated by
Susan Davis

TIME-LIFE FOR CHILDREN
ALEXANDRIA, VIRGINIA

The sun slowly slips away,
leaving twinkling stars above.

The turtle is sleeping
at the pond.
It rests under a fallen log,
safe inside its shell.

The fish are sleeping in the river.
Eyes wide open, they float silently
near the river bottom.

The flowers are sleeping
in the meadow.
They fold up their petals
in the cool night air.

The squirrel is sleeping
in the woods.
High in a tree, it lies quiet and
cozy in its bed of leaves.

The bees are sleeping
in the hive.
They gently buzz
inside their
humming home.

The rabbit is sleeping
in the field.
It naps in a hollow beneath
a blanket of green grass.

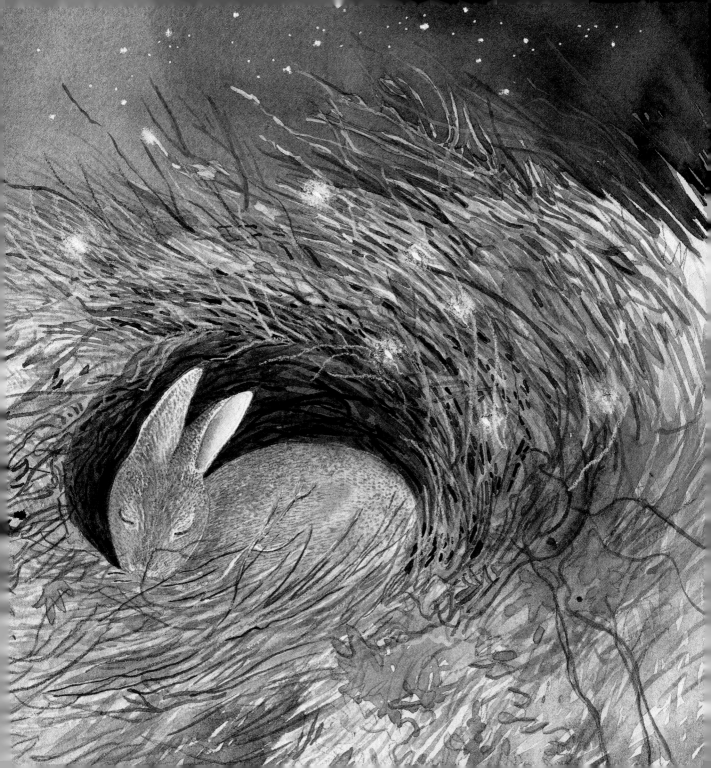

The bird is sleeping
in the tree.
It tucks its tiny head
into its warm,
feathery body.

The dog is sleeping on the porch.
It stretches and dozes peacefully
in the moonlight.

The cat is sleeping
on the steps.
Curled into a fuzzy ball,
it softly purrs.

The child is sleeping
in the bed,
cuddled and snuggled
in the warm covers.

**Good night.
Sleep tight!**